# Kingdom Kicks Series
# A Lesson on Courtesy

Written by Ginny Tyler

Scripture taken from the Common English Bible ®, CEB® Copyright © 2010, 2011 by Common English Bible. ™
Used by permission.  All rights reserved worldwide.  The "CEB" and "Common English Bible" trademarks are
registered in the United States Patent and Trademark Office by Common English Bible.  Use of either trademark
requires the permission of Common English Bible.

ISBN: 1974292002
ISBN-13: 978-1974292004

# DEDICATION

This book is dedicated to all of the Kingdom Warriors in this world.  We all have a part to play, and however small it seems to be we are working towards the same ultimate goal.

1 Corinthians 12:4-11

Glory to God, who is able to do far beyond all that we could ask or imagine by his power at work within us.


Ephesians 3:20

## ACKNOWLEDGMENTS

I would first like to thank my husband, Joe, without whom any of this would be possible.  I am truly blessed to have you in my life.  Thank you, Coco, for all of your help.  Thank you to my HSS and friends, who offered encouragement on this venture. I would also like to thank my instructor, Keith Yates, for starting me on the path that led to where I am now.  If you had not invested in my martial arts training, none of this would have come to fruition.

I am incredibly grateful for all of you.

Class was wrapping up at DMD Martial arts, but today the dojo was silent, save for the voice of Sensei.  All of the students were intently listening as he spoke.

"Students, we begin and end every class with a bow.  Not only does it demonstrate respect, but can you think of a tenet that we are practicing?"

Hands flew up.  "Integrity!" Michael called out.

"Possibly, Michael," the instructor answered, "but there is a better one.  And everyone, please wait for me to call on you before answering.  Ian?"

"Humility, Sensei?"

"Getting warmer... it does demonstrate humility.  But I'm thinking of a different one.  Elizabeth?"

"Courtesy?"

"Very good, Elizabeth.  That's what I was thinking, too", Sensei said with a smile.

"You see, students, Proverbs 3:27 says, 'Don't withhold good from someone who deserves it, when it is in your power to do so.'  Now, does the Bible mean for us to only show courtesy to those we deem deserving?  To those who can benefit us somehow?"

"No way!" called Eliana.  The other students murmured in agreement.

The Lord will be your confidence; he will guard your feet from being snared.

Proverbs 3:27 Don't withhold good from someone who deserves it, when it is in your power to do so.

Don't say to your neighbor, "Go and come back; I'll give it to you tomorrow," when you have it. Don't plan to harm your neighbor who trusts and lives near you. Don't accuse anyone without reason, when they haven't harmed you. Don't envy violent people or choose any of their ways."

"You're right, Eliana.  You know students, there is a story in Genesis 18, verses 1-15, and in this story, Abraham was resting by his tent when three strangers approached him.  He did not nod them by as they passed, and he did not ignore them.  Rather, he showed them courtesy."

"He bowed to them, much like we bow to each other.  He brought them water to wash their feet, then had his wife prepare a feast.  He did not bring out old food, rather, he treated them to freshly baked bread, meat cooked just for them, butter and milk.  Abraham demonstrated courtesy to these strangers by serving his finest to them.  Does anyone know what happened next?"

The students looked deep in thought, but no hands raised.

"The strangers that came to see Abraham were really angels in disguise. I wonder how Abraham would have felt, had he not treated these strangers with courtesy, only to find out after they left that they were sent by God Himself?"

Sensei looked around the room at the wide eyes of his students, then continued. "In fact, Hebrews 13:2 even says, 'Don't neglect to open up your homes to guests, because by doing this some have been hosts to angels without knowing it'. Courtesy is such a beautiful tenet, because often you don't realize the change you bring into the world when you show it. And, like a cold, it does tend to be contagious. So, my challenge to all of you this week is to demonstrate courtesy to those around you. Can you do that?"

"Yes, sir!" the students echoed loudly.

"Very good. Let's bow out."

As Elizabeth made her way out of class that day, she resolved to demonstrate courtesy to everyone around her for that week.

'Maybe I can change the world!' she thought to herself.  She grinned at the thought as she devised ways to show kindness to her family, friends, and maybe even strangers!

That night at home, she set and cleared the table for her mother, without being asked to.  She even washed the dishes!

"Oh Elizabeth, what a wonderful surprise!" her mother exclaimed.  "Thank you so much, sweet girl."

Motivated to keep the momentum going, Elizabeth helped her little brother clean his room that evening.  Then the following day, she brought in the newspaper for her dad, and left it at his place at the table.  Unfortunately, he had left early for work that morning, so she didn't get to see his response.

At school, she held doors open for students as a courtesy – she was even late to her first class because of it!

She helped younger students clean up their messes at lunch, and at the end of the day, she offered to help her last teacher, Mrs. Miller, carry her supplies to her car. "What a blessing you are, Elizabeth!" Mrs. Miller told her. Elizabeth felt appreciated, but she wondered if she was really making a difference in the world.

After school, she walked to her church to help with service projects. They were stuffing bears to send to children in Romania. Elizabeth wasn't the best at sewing but she tried her best, convinced that a little courtesy is better than no courtesy. She even offered to come back the following day to help package meals to send to Africa!

The next day was much like the last. Elizabeth did her best to demonstrate courtesy to those around her, but again, she wondered how much good she was truly doing. At lunch time, as she pondered this, she noticed the new girl, Olivia, in the corner of the lunch room. What caught her attention was a group of girls standing around her, seemingly teasing her. Well, that's what their tone, and Olivia's face suggested anyway.

Elizabeth made her way over, thinking, 'I would sure hate to be Olivia right now. New in school AND being made fun of.' As she approached the group of girls, the leader of the bunch, Amy, glared at Elizabeth and said, "What are *you* doing here, Elizabeth?" The girls standing around Amy casually walked away, giggling.

Now that she was closer, Elizabeth could see that Olivia had tears in her eyes. "I just came to spend some time with my new friend, Olivia." Then she turned to Olivia, "Sorry I'm late, I got caught up in that lunch line."

Olivia looked surprised by Elizabeth's response, and her eyes darted back to Amy.

"I don't know why you'd want to spend lunch with her, Elizabeth, she's just a book worm."

Elizabeth retorted, "You know, Amy, God loves her, and me, and even you, more than anything. I just wish you knew that inside so that you wouldn't feel like you had to hurt other people's feelings."

Amy jerked back slightly, narrowing her eyes at Elizabeth. "Yea, well...", she trailed off. It seemed like she didn't know what else to say, so she made a snort noise, rolled her eyes, and left the table.

Olivia looked at Elizabeth in wonder. "Why did you do that?"

"Because it's true, Olivia."

"Where did you learn that?"

"My church", Elizabeth answered. "I'm going there tonight to help package some meals, want to come with me?"

Olivia's face brightened. "I'd love to", she whispered. "Thank you."

That afternoon, the girls went to Elizabeth's church to package meals.  They got to know each other much better than they had in school, and in fact, after that afternoon they stayed very good friends.  Olivia even began visiting Elizabeth's church with her family over the years.  But even she will tell you that her very best friendship started that day in the school lunch room.

However, when Elizabeth came back to the dojo the following week, she seemed somewhat disheartened after class.  Sensei had noticed during their workout, but he had thought maybe it was due to the dreary weather.  It had been raining all day, after all.  "Sensei, may I please talk to you for a minute?" she asked after everyone bowed out.

"Yes, of course, Elizabeth.  What's on your mind?"

"This week, I really tried to demonstrate courtesy.  I did so many things, and I really wanted to make the world a better place.  You say we have to be the change we want to see, but I didn't see any change."

"Aah, Elizabeth.  I'm so proud of you for your efforts", Sensei began.  "But oftentimes, as I mentioned, we don't even realize the scope of the goodness we have done – or if we do, perhaps it comes much later.  How do you know you haven't done any good?"

"Well, I just don't think I did.  I can't tell."

Sensei looked out the window at the drizzling rain for a moment, then a smile grew on his face.  "Come over here for a moment, Elizabeth", he said as he walked her towards the front of the dojo.

"What do you see?"

"Rain."

"I see the world", the instructor replied. He walked over to the door and opened it. "Sometimes God speaks to us in a way that we don't understand. Sometimes we just need to keep our eyes open and wait."

Elizabeth looked at the sky. She saw clouds, and... wait. What was that? A faint hue of color was just beginning to appear ahead of her gaze. "I think I see a..", she began excitedly, looking at Sensei.

He nodded to her. "Keep watching."

Over the next few minutes, the color grew in clarity, as well as hue variation, until, before the instructor and Elizabeth knew it, there was a half arch of rainbow stretching from one puffy cloud to another.

Elizabeth's face lit up as Sensei said, "I think God is telling you something."

Elizabeth never forgot what happened that afternoon at DMD Martial Arts.  And over the years, as her friends began to move away, including Olivia, she remained in her home town to stay close to her family, church, and what meant most to her.

In fact, one day at church, she sat eagerly waiting for services to begin.  A dark-skinned woman sat beside her that she had never seen before, so she turned to the woman to offer her a welcome. The woman smiled a beautiful smile at Elizabeth, as she shook her hand and said, "Good morning."

"Good morning," Elizabeth said. "Are you new to our church?"
"Oh, I'm just passing through and had to visit. I feel like I know the place already, from all I've heard of it back home."
"And where is home?"
"Africa", the woman said with a broad smile.
Elizabeth was puzzled. "Well," she said, "it's a shame I won't get a chance to know you better." She felt as if she knew this woman somehow...
"We have all of eternity for that", the woman replied, looking towards the front as the band began to play.

Elizabeth nodded and smiled to herself.  She meant to at least get the woman's name, but as soon as services were over, she seemed to have slipped out without her seeing.  Wondering what happened to the curious stranger, Elizabeth shrugged and went to greet friends a few rows ahead.

But what Elizabeth didn't know was that this woman was brought to Christ by a missionary in her small town.  This missionary had, in fact, travelled all over the globe from Romania, to Spain, to Ecuador, the Ukraine, and yes, Africa, too.  This missionary gave her life to Christ because a seed was planted many years ago – a seed that taught her the lesson that a simple act of courtesy could change the outcome of a person's life.  This missionary's name was Olivia, and the woman who sat beside Elizabeth was the fruit of her selfless act as a child.

She just didn't know it.

# Glossary of Japanese Martial Arts Terms

Do – The Way

Dojo – Karate School

Domo Arigato – Many Thanks

Gi – Uniform

Hai – Yes

Hajime – "Begin" Command

Karate-Do – Way of Empty Hand

Karate-ka – Student

Kata – Forms

Oss – Respectful Greeting (alternatively "osu", but commonly used as oss to depict pronunciation)

Rei – Bow

Senpai – Senior Belt

Sensei – Literally, "the one who has gone before."  Commonly used to mean Teacher

Seiretsu – Line Up

Seiza – Sitting at Attention

Yame – "Stop" Command

## Counting to 10 in Japanese:
Ichi

Ni

San

Shi

Go

Roku

Shichi

Hachi

Ku

Ju

For exclusive Parent/Instructor bonus content, please visit www.dmdtaekwondo.com

# ABOUT THE AUTHOR

Ginny Aversa Tyler is a wife and homeschooling mother of three children.
She is the owner and founder of DMD Tae Kwon Do, a Christian martial arts school near
McKinney, Texas. (www.dmdtaekwondo.com)

Inspired by the endless lessons both God's Word and the martial arts have to offer, Ginny
created the Kingdom Kicks book series for children so that they may tie their love of the
martial arts to the lifelong guidance our Heavenly Father has offered.

Ginny's passion for teaching, not just her own children and students, is the basis for the
Kingdom Kicks series, through which she wishes to inspire children all over the world to seek
Biblical truths outside the walls of their home, school, and martial arts classes.

Made in the USA
Middletown, DE
21 November 2017